The Vexing

Hectare Detector

**Written & Illustrated
by Ken Bowser**

Solving Mysteries Through
Science, Technology, Engineering, Art & Math

RED CHAIR
PRESS
•PRESS•

Egremont, Massachusetts

The Jesse Steam Mysteries are produced and published by:
Red Chair Press LLC   PO Box 333   South Egremont, MA 01258-0333
www.redchairpress.com

FREE Educator Guide at www.redchairpress.com/free-resources

For My Grandson, Liam

Publisher's Cataloging-In-Publication Data
Names: Bowser, Ken, author, illustrator.
Title: The vexing hectare detector / written & illustrated by Ken Bowser.
Other Titles: Hectare detector

Description: South Egremont, MA : Red Chair Press, [2021] | Series: A
    Jesse Steam mystery | "Solving Mysteries Through Science, Technology,
    Engineering, Art & Math." | Includes a word list and hands-on
    Makerspace activity. | Interest age level: 008-011. | Summary: "It's
    Spring Break at Deanville Elementary School and the gang are presented
    with a mysterious new riddle that will challenge their mathematics
    skills and senses. What is the perplexing, suspended ring that
    oscillates?"-- Provided by publisher.

Identifiers: ISBN 9781643710242 (library hardcover) | ISBN 9781643710259
    (paperback) | ISBN 9781643710266 (ebook)

Subjects: LCSH: Swings--Juvenile fiction. | Measurement--Juvenile fiction.
    | Pythagorean theorem--Juvenile fiction. | CYAC: Swings--Fiction. |
    Measurement--Fiction. | Pythagorean theorem--Fiction. | LCGFT:
    Detective and mystery fiction.

Classification: LCC PZ7.B697 Ve 2021 (print) | LCC PZ7.B697 (ebook) | DDC
    [Fic]--dc23

LC record available at https://lccn.loc.gov/2020934641

Printed in the United States of America

0920 1P CGS21

Table of Contents

Cast of Characters
Meet Jesse, Mr. Stubbs & The Gang   4

Town Map
Find Your Way Around Deanville   6

Chapter 1
One Giant Leap for Cat-kind   8

Chapter 2
Pythago Who? 16

Chapter 3
Voila! The Riddle of The Rock 22

Chapter 4
Hey Diddle, Diddle. Miss Byrd Has a Riddle 28

Chapter 5
Time to Define 34

Chapter 6
Mapmaker, Mapmaker, Make Me a Map 42

Chapter 7
A Map to Nowhere 48

Chapter 8
One Giant Leap for Frog-kind 56

Jesse's Word List 62

Makerspace Activity: Try It Out! 64

Cast of Characters

Jesse Steam

Amateur sleuth and all-around neat kid. Jesse loves riding her bike, solving mysteries, and most of all, Mr. Stubbs. Jesse is never without her messenger bag and the cool stuff it holds.

Mr. Stubbs

A cat with an attitude, he's the coolest tabby cat in Deanville. Stubbs was a stray cat who strayed right into Jesse's heart. Can you figure out how he got his name?

Professor Peach

A retired university professor. Professor Peach knows tons of cool stuff and is somewhat of a legend in Deanville. He has college degrees in Science, Technology, Engineering, Art, and Math.

Emmett

Professor Peach's ever-present pet, white lab rat. He loves cheese balls, and wherever you find The Professor, you're sure to find Emmett—even though he might be difficult to spot!

Clark & Lewis

Jesse's next-door neighbor and sometimes formidable adversary, Clark Johnson, and his slippery, slimy, gross-looking pet frog, Lewis. Yuck.

Dorky Dougy

Clark Johnson's three-year-old, tag-along baby brother. Dougy is never without his stuffed alligator, a rubber knife, and something really goofy to say, like "eleventy-seven."

Kimmy Kat Black

Holder of the Deanville Elementary School Long Jump Record, know-it-all, and self-proclaimed future member of Mensa. Kimmy Kat Black lives near the Spooky Tree.

Liam LePoole

A black belt in karate and also the captain of the Deanville Community Swimming Pool Cannonball Team. Liam's best friend is Chompy Dog, his stinky, gassy, and frenzied, brown puggle.

Miss Byrd

Everyone's favorite teacher and all-around cool person. Miss Byrd was named teacher of the year at Deanville Elementary School three years in a row!

Pythagoras

Born on the Greek island of Samos in the eastern Aegean Sea in 570 BC. That was a REALLY long time ago. He was super-smart and studied all kinds of complicated stuff.

The Town of Deanville

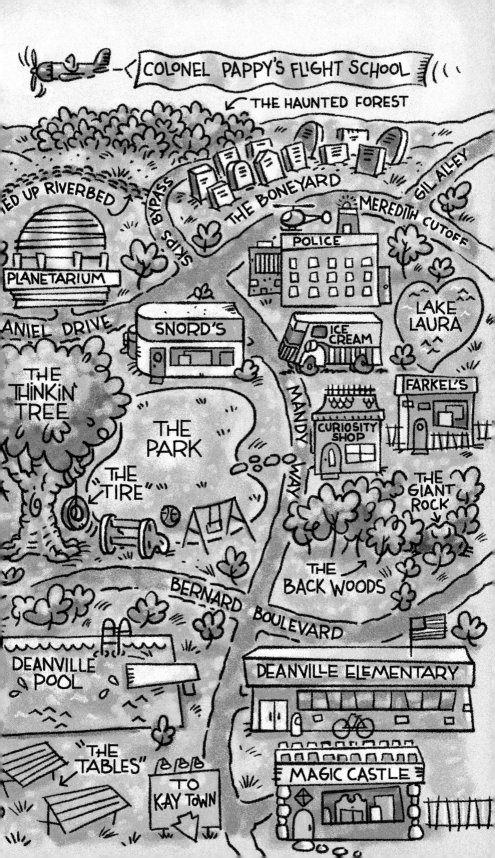

One Giant Leap for Cat-kind

Chapter 1

"Don't you just love springtime, Mr. Stubbs?" Jesse asked her cat, who was sitting on the floor at her feet. Stubbs was silently pondering a grasshopper that had just landed on his nose from the open window.

"Warmer weather. Flowers blooming. Fresh air and chirping birds." Jesse drew a deep breath from her bedroom window. "Ahhhh," she sighed.

"Not to mention the fact that today is the last day of school before we have two glorious weeks off for spring break," Jesse went on talking to Stubbs.

Jesse continued talking while she packed her messenger bag with the things that she was going to need for the day. She never went anywhere without her messenger bag and the important things that it held.

"Let's see," she said. "My teacher, Miss Byrd, said that she was going to give us a fun riddle to solve over spring break that would involve math, maps, and measurements. So, I think I had better pack my measuring tape," she said as she placed it in her bag.

"A ruler is always a handy thing to have as well. Along with a calculator and something to write in, like my journal." Jesse was never without her journal.

"Packing a town map of Deanville is a good idea. Miss Byrd said that the riddle would involve maps, so I really need to bring this along, too."

Jesse continued to fill her messenger bag with the regular things while Stubbs continued to contemplate the grasshopper that remained perched on his nose.

"Magnifying glass. Check. Pen and pencils. Check. Compass. Check." Jesse continued to fill her bag.

"Bike lock. Check." Jesse went on checking things off of her list as she placed them into her messenger bag.

At that very moment, Jesse's concentration was broken by Mr. Stubbs' sudden leap from his spot on the floor. He

jumped straight up in the air, chasing the grasshopper and landed practically all the way across the room on the top of Jesse's tallest dresser. "Whoa! Good jump, Stubby!" Jesse praised the cat at his amazing feat. "That has to be a new personal record for

you, dude! Let's measure it and see how far you jumped!" Jesse pulled the measuring tape from her messenger bag. "Let's see," Jesse started.

"From your spot on the floor to the front of the dresser is..." Jesse stretched the measuring tape slowly across the floor. "Thirty-six inches. Or, three feet."

Jesse continued to measure. "Now, the dresser, from the floor to the top where you landed, is forty-eight inches tall. Or, four feet."

Mr. Stubbs watched as Jesse continued. "So, let's measure how far you went in the air." Jesse began to measure from the spot on the floor where Stubbs started to where he landed on the dresser. "Oh no. My tape measure is only four feet long, so I can't find this third measurement!" Jesse said in frustration.

"I guess we'll have to wait until we have a longer tape measure to see what your new record is."

Chapter 2

"Why don't you just ask Pythagoras?" Jesse heard a familiar voice coming from behind her.

"Kimmy! You scared me half to death." Jesse turned to see Kimmy Kat Black at the window. "What did you just say?" Jesse asked.

Kimmy repeated herself. "I said, why don't you just ask Pythagoras? I watched as you tried to find that third measurement, but your tape measure was too short. Why don't you just ask Pythagoras for some help?" Kimmy went on.

Jesse looked at Kimmy like she had rotten cheeseburgers coming out of her ears. "What in the world are you talking about, Kimmy? You know, sometimes you make absolutely no sense at all."

Kimmy kept talking. "Pythagoras was the Greek philosopher who gave us the Pythagorean theorem," she said with a smirk. She had a way of being really smirky.

"As a genuine genius and a future member of Mensa, I like to keep on top of all things Pythagorean." Kimmy never let a minute go by without letting you know just how smart she was.

"You see," she went on, "Pythagoras taught us that the square of the length of the hypotenuse of a right triangle equals the sum of the squares of the lengths of the other two sides."

More rotten cheeseburgers.

"In other words," Kimmy continued, "if we know the length of two of the sides of the triangle, we can figure out the length of the third side with a formula. We use the formula, $a^2 + b^2 = c^2$. This is Pythagoras' formula or theorem. A right angle is the 'L'

shaped angle that is where your floor and dresser meet." Kimmy continued. "The hypotenuse is the path or angle that was made by Stubbs when he leapt from his spot on the floor to the top of the dresser," Kimmy said with a smug look on her face.

"Now, we know that one side of the right angle is 3 feet. So, we 'square' that. 3 × 3 = 9. And we know that the other side of the right angle is 4 feet. We square that. 4 × 4 = 16. Now we add those two numbers together. 9 + 16 = 25. The last step in finding the third measurement is to find the square root of 25. So, what number times itself equals 25?"

Jesse thought for a while. "Hmmm." She paused. "Wait! I've got it! The answer is 5! 5 × 5 = 25! The length of the hypotenuse is five feet! Did you hear that, Mr. Stubbs? A new record! You jumped five feet!"

Stubbs just purred and contemplated the grasshopper that was now on his nose.

Voila! The Riddle of The Rock

Chapter 3

Jesse finished packing her messenger bag. Waving goodbye to Stubbs, she and Kimmy Kat Black headed off to school on their bikes.

They turned the corner and headed up and over The Creepy Bridge that traversed Bruce Spring Stream as they pedaled toward Deanville Elementary.

"Do you know how far it is from The Creepy Bridge to the school?" Kimmy asked Jesse.

"I have no idea, Kimmy," Jesse replied. "How in the world would I possibly know that? And why should I even care?"

"Well, I know," Kimmy Kat snapped back with a sneer. "I have personally deduced that it is approximately three-quarters of a mile. Or three thousand nine hundred sixty feet, to be more precise," she said smugly.

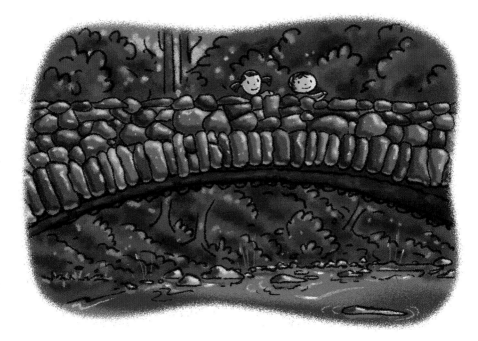

Kimmy Kat Black was always deducing something—precisely.

"And how did you deduce that so precisely?" Jesse mocked back.

"Simple! I timed myself every day for a week as I walked to school, starting at The Creepy Bridge. Each time it took me almost exactly fifteen minutes. Some times were a few seconds longer. Some a bit shorter. But, each time it took me basically fifteen minutes."

"Go on," Jesse said.

"Then, I did some simple research and learned that the average person walks three miles per hour. And while I'm not merely average in any other way, I figure I'm a pretty average walker. Which means that in fifteen minutes I walked three-quarters of a mile. Now, we know that a mile is 5,289 feet, right? So, I just used my calculator and determined that three-quarters of a mile is 3,960 feet. Voila!" Kimmy loved to say *voila* even though it was the only French word that she knew.

"That's how far it is from The Creepy Bridge to the school!"

"Well, aren't you something else," Jesse said with a chuckle.

As Jesse and Kimmy rode up to the school, they noticed the regular gang gathered around a big poster.

Liam LePoole was there and so was Clark Johnson with his pet frog, Lewis, peeking out from Clark's backpack. And of course, Clark's tag-along little brother, Dorky Dougy was there too.

"What do we have here, kids?" Jesse asked the group.

"It's The Riddle of The Rock," Liam LePoole answered as the rest of the kids looked on. "You remember. Miss Byrd told us all about it last week."

"Oh yeah!" Jesse and Kimmy said in unison.

Chapter 4

As Jesse sat in her classroom, she gazed out through the large picture window by her desk. She couldn't help but daydream about all of the things that she and Kimmy Kat Black had discussed that morning. Even though Kimmy could be a bit annoying, she was really smart and had a knack for math.

"Class," Miss Byrd's voice broke the silence in Jesse's head as she popped out of her daydream.

"Before we leave for Spring Break, I want to discuss The Riddle of The Rock that you've heard about all week," she continued.

"Now, it's not mandatory, but I encourage all of you to take part if you can.

It's fun, very educational, and it will get you outside and away from your televisions and video games for a change," she said with a smile. The entire class laughed.

"Plus," she continued, "whoever solves the riddle and brings back The Riddle Rock wins something that the entire class can enjoy!"

Miss Byrd held up a large, rolled-up parchment. "I have one of these beautiful parchment scrolls for each of you to take home and study."

She unrolled the parchment and read the riddle aloud so the entire class could hear:

"You'll need to stroll through country fare,
traversing this green, one-hundred are.
And once you do you'll find what waits
—the suspended ring that oscillates.
Four rods due west is next you'll walk
in search of one large, heart-shaped rock.
Beneath the stone the spoils are found.

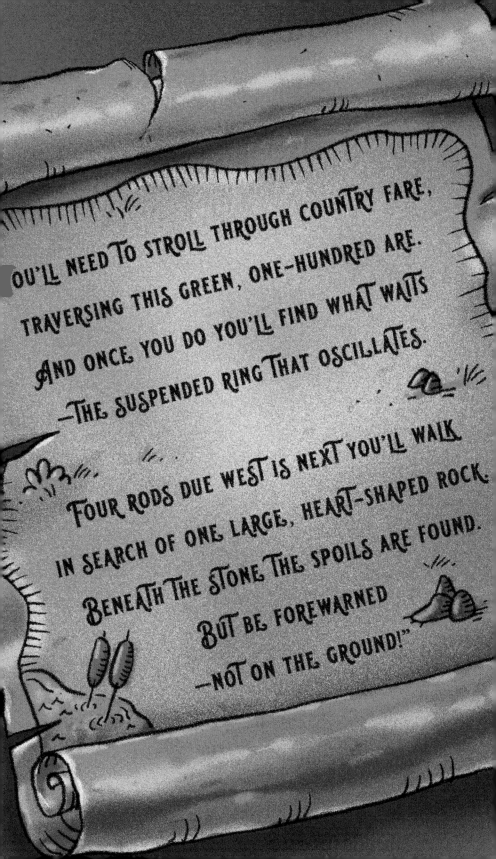

OU'LL NEED TO STROLL THROUGH COUNTRY FARE,
TRAVERSING THIS GREEN, ONE-HUNDRED ARE.
AND ONCE YOU DO YOU'LL FIND WHAT WAITS
—THE SUSPENDED RING THAT OSCILLATES.

FOUR RODS DUE WEST IS NEXT YOU'LL WALK
IN SEARCH OF ONE LARGE, HEART-SHAPED ROCK.
BENEATH THE STONE THE SPOILS ARE FOUND.
BUT BE FOREWARNED
—NOT ON THE GROUND!"

But be forewarned

—not on the ground!"

The kids gazed at one another with puzzled looks on their faces.

"What in the world does that all mean?" Jesse whispered over to Kimmy Kat Black who looked just as puzzled as the rest of the kids.

"I don't even know!" Kimmy said. "It sounded like a bunch of gibberish to me, and I'm a genius!"

On the way home, Jesse, Kimmy, and the rest of the gang stopped at The Thinkin' Tree to discuss the riddle. Kimmy studied her map. Jesse hung upside down from the tree like she always does when she's trying to figure something out, while Clark and Dougy played with Lewis.

Liam LePoole spun on the tire swing and said to the group, "A suspended ring that oscillates! What in the world could that be?"

Time to Define

Chapter 5

"What do we have here?" Professor Peach asked Jesse as she rode up on her bicycle.

The Professor was Jesse's next-door neighbor and had advanced degrees in Science, Technology, Engineering, Art, and Math. He was always a good source of information when Jesse was stuck on a particularly tricky problem or puzzle.

Jesse unrolled the scroll and read the riddle out loud to him.

"Ah! A riddle!" The Professor exclaimed. "I love a good riddle, and this sounds like a doozy. Would you like me to help you solve it?" he asked.

"That would be great," Jesse returned. "But I really need to do this on my own. It's kind of a class assignment," she went on, "but, I would take a few words of advice if you have any to offer."

"Well, my dear," The Professor said, "in that case, I would start with a good dictionary to help you define some of the words or phrases that have you stumped. And, considering the riddle involves finding something outside, creating a hand-drawn map might be the next logical step."

"Great idea!" Jesse said, and she went straight to work on solving The Riddle of The Rock.

Jesse settled in at the desk in her bedroom and opened her biggest dictionary. "Let's start with this first part of the riddle," she said to Stubbs, who was now by her side. She read it out loud—"'Traversing this green, one-hundred are.'"

"I already know that *traverse* means to cross, but what is a 'green, one-hundred are'?" Jesse looked up the word *are* in her dictionary. "Ah, ha! Here it is! The second

definition of the word *are* in this dictionary reads: 'a metric unit of measure, equal to 100 square meters'. And it rhymes with *air* not *car*. That's a great start!"

Jesse went on to learn that 100 ares is a hectare, and a hectare is about the size of two football fields. "So, we're looking for a green, outdoor area that's about the size of two football fields. Like the park by The Thinkin' Tree! That's it!"

Jesse read the next line in the riddle. "'A suspended ring that oscillates.' Well,

suspend means to hang. We know that. And a ring can be anything shaped like a ring."

Jesse looked up the word *oscillate*. Its definition read: "to move or swing back and forth." Jesse thought for a while. "So, we're looking for a hanging ring shape, that swings back and forth, and is near the park. The tire swing! That's it!" Jesse shouted out loud.

"Now, for the next part of the riddle," Jesse said to Stubbs. "'Four rods due west.'"

Jesse looked up the word *rod* in her dictionary. "Here it is," she nudged Stubbs. "The third definition in my dictionary says that a rod is 'a linear measure, especially for land, equal to 5.5 yards.'" Jesse closed her dictionary.

"Well, it looks like our work has just begun, Stubby, old boy," she said to Mr. Stubbs, who was now sound asleep on Jesse's desk.

"We're looking for a rock that is four rods due west of the tire swing. Time to do some reconnaissance and draw our map!"

Mapmaker, Mapmaker, Make Me a Map

Chapter 6

Jesse began to gather up some art supplies to pack into her messenger bag.

"Let's see. First of all, I think I'll need my sketchbook. Some crayons and markers next. A ruler is a good idea, and of course, I'll bring a tape measure."

After packing, Jesse headed to the park with Stubbs in his usual spot—the basket on the front of her bike. It was a beautiful spring day, and Jesse caught the smell of fresh-cut grass coming from the big park.

"Where ya headed, Jesse Gal?"

Kimmy Kat Black called out as Jesse rode by on her bike. Kimmy was sitting on the stone wall of The Creepy Bridge and tossing stones into Bruce Spring Stream below.

"Oh, just to the park," Jesse answered.

"Great! I'll join ya." Kimmy smiled as

she hopped down from her perch on the stone wall.

"So, what're you doing at the park today, Jess?" Kimmy was always so inquisitive. Or she was just nosy. Jesse could never really tell for certain with Kimmy.

Not wanting to let anyone in on the fact that she was working on the riddle, Jesse simply replied, "Oh, I thought I'd just sit and do a few landscape drawings. You know, it's so pretty out today." Jesse loved to draw, so that was nothing out of the ordinary.

"Oh. Cool," is all Kimmy had to say about that. "I'll just hang out on the tire swing while you draw."

"You mean the suspended ring that oscillates," Jesse whispered to herself under her breath with a chuckle.

Jesse sat in the freshly cut grass by The Thinkin' Tree and surveyed the area around her. The park was huge, but it seemed even

bigger now that she knew it covered an entire hectare.

In her sketchbook, Jesse began to map out her surroundings. She started by drawing the entire shape of the park. On her sketch she noted where The Thinkin' Tree was, along with other notable objects. She noted the position of The Creepy Bridge, The Secret Clearing, and Bruce Spring Stream in between.

Using her compass, she found true north and drew a compass rose on her map as well.

"There," she said to Stubbs when she was done. "We can finish this at home and then come back tomorrow to search for The Riddle Rock."

Chapter 7

The next morning arrived, and Jesse sat down and completed her final map from the sketch she had made in the park, trying her best to make it as accurate as possible.

"Stubby, old boy, I think we're ready to try and solve this riddle once and for all. Let's head out on the bike."

It was another beautiful day in Deanville, so there was a lot of activity at the big park and around The Thinkin' Tree.

"Let's park the bike at Snord's Gas Station and walk into the park the back way, so we don't draw too much attention to ourselves," she whispered to Stubbs. "We don't want the others knowing we're working on the riddle."

Jesse studied her map again, and using her compass, she faced west. She looked at her map as she held the compass out in front of her and Stubbs. "Okay. four rods straight ahead." Jesse pulled out her tape measure. "Only one problem, Stubbs." She laughed. "Our tape measure is only four feet long, and one rod is five and a half yards. So, four rods is twenty-two yards! Now what? I have an idea," Jesse said.

With her tape measure, she marked out three feet or, a length equal to one yard, on the ground and marked the distance with two rocks. "Alright. Let's see." Jesse took

two normal steps. "One yard. Two of my steps equal one yard. So, that means that four rods is forty-four of my steps!"

Map in hand, Jesse began counting off forty-four steps, keeping an eye on her compass all the while.

"There," she said to Stubbs, who was by her side the entire time. "forty-four steps."

Jesse looked around. To her right was the group of trees that encircled The Secret Clearing. To her left was The Creepy Bridge, and right in front of her was shallow Bruce Spring Stream. But no heart-shaped rock.

Jesse recited the last line of The Riddle of The Rock again.

"'Beneath the stone the spoils are found. But be forewarned—not on the ground!'"

"Not on the ground. Not on the ground," Jesse repeated the mysterious phrase over and over again.

"What could that mean? Not on the

ground?" Jesse looked around. "Well, if it's not on the ground, then where could it be?"

"Up in a tree? In a bush? On The Creepy Bridge? Up in the sky?"

Jesse walked into The Secret Clearing—a circle of trees that surrounded a small, open grassy area.

"This is always a great spot for a picnic, but it's way more than forty-four steps from the tire swing. No sense in even looking here." She walked over to The Creepy Bridge.

"Kimmy Kat Black was sitting here just yesterday. If the heart-shaped rock was over here on the bridge, she would have surely found it," she mumbled to Stubbs.

"Now what, Stubbs? We've come way too far to just give up now."

"I need a break..."

One Giant Leap for Frog-kind

Chapter 8

Jesse plopped down on the bank of Bruce Spring Stream to rest and soothe her tired feet in its cool, clear water.

"We figured out all of the equations. We followed all of the clues, and we solved the meaning of the oscillating ring. All of that. Only to hit a dead end after traversing, who knows how many rods and hectares. Looking for a rock that's not on the ground." Jesse sighed.

"Ribbit!"

"Did you say something, Stubbs?" Jesse asked.

"Ribbit!" She heard the sound again. Jesse turned just in time to see Mr. Stubbs chasing after a giant bullfrog by the stream.

"Ribbit!" The giant frog croaked once more. "Stubbs, leave that poor frog alone you crazy cat."

"Ribbit!" The frog croaked one last time before taking a giant leap into the stream, sending a huge splash of water onto Jesse and Stubbs.

The commotion cleared, and Jesse looked down in the still-swirling water of Bruce Spring Stream. She looked at the frog. The frog looked back. Jesse looked back at the frog again—who was sitting on a rock. A heart-shaped rock. A shiny, beautiful, heart-shaped rock!

"Well, well, Mr. Frog. What do we have here?" Jesse reached down into the shallow water and retrieved the heart-shaped rock. Turning it over, she read the writing painted on the bottom. It read:

FREE PIZZA PARTY
TO THE BEARER OF THIS ROCK
—MISS BYRD

Jesse could only laugh. "Well, it wasn't on the ground after all now was it, Stubbs! It was in the water all along!"

Spring Break came to an end at Deanville Elementary School, and with the help of a big dictionary, one ornery orange cat, a slimy green frog, and Pythagoras, Jesse Steam had solved The Riddle of The Rock.

It was a good day in Deanville.

Ribbit.

THE END.

Jesse's Word List

Accurate
correct—*It was accurate that he had bad breath.*

Annoying
irritating—*His bad breath was annoying.*

Doozy
unique—*His bad breath was a doozy!*

Feat
something done with great strength—*Avoiding his breath was a feat.*

Gazed
look intently—*I gazed at his rotten teeth.*

Nosy
keenly curious—*I was nosy about his teeth.*

Notable
remarkable—*His breath was notable.*

Ponder
think about—*I pondered his bad breath.*

Rotten
decayed—*Yep. His teeth were rotten.*

Smirk
a sly smile—*I smirked at his yucky teeth.*

Smug
showing excessive pride—*I was smug about my clean teeth.*

Sneer
to mock—like when someone makes fun of the man with bad breath

Soothe
to calm—*I will soothe his hurt feelings.*

Stumped
puzzled—*I was stumped when I couldn't soothe him.*

Toss
throw—*I tried not to toss my lunch.*

Traverse
travel—*I traversed the room.*

Unison
together—*My friends traversed in unison.*

Voila
an exclamation—*Voila! We were gone!*

About the Author & Illustrator

Ken Bowser is an illustrator and writer whose work has appeared in hundreds of books and countless periodicals. While he's been drawing for as long as he could hold a pencil, all of his work today is created digitally on a computer. He works out of his home studio in Central Florida with his wife Laura and a big, lazy, orange cat.

Try It Out!

Learn About Measures and Units

In *The Vexing Hectare Detector*, Jesse Steam solved "The Riddle of The Rock" by using her tape measure and some terms and definitions that she learned from her dictionary. You can do some of the same calculations that Jesse did with just a few items that you may already have at home.

What You Need: A tape measure—the longer the better. A 20 foot tape measure would be best, but even a simple ruler will work. A pencil and something to write notes on. A small hand-held calculator. You can do the calculations without a calculator if you have strong math skills, but a calculator makes it easier.

Steps:

1. Start with something simple, like your kitchen table.

2. Measure the length of the tabletop and note it on your paper. It's easiest if you round up to "feet" while you're first learning the process. For example, if your table-top is three feet, ten inches long, just round up to four feet.

3. Measure the width and note it on your paper. Round up to feet as you did in step 2.

4. Using your calculator, multiply one measurement by the other. For example, if your tabletop was four feet by five feet you just multiply 4 × 5 which equals 20! You've just learned that the top of your kitchen table is 20 square feet!

Now you have the skills to find the square foot or square inch measurements of anything you like. Even something as big as your entire room. Or your whole house!